HANS CHRISTIAN ANDERSEN

THUMBELINE

Copyright © 1980 by NordSüd Verlag AG, Zürich, Switzerland.
First published in Switzerland under the title *Däumelinchen*.
English translation copyright © 1985 by North-South Books Inc.

First published in the United States, Great Britain, Canada,
Australia, and New Zealand in 2000 by North-South Books,
an imprint of NordSüd Verlag AG, Zürich, Switzerland.

Distributed in the United States by North-South Books Inc., New York

Library of Congress Cataloging-in-Publication Data is available.
A CIP catalogue record for this book is available from The British Library.

ISBN 978-0-7358-2236-8 (paperback) 10 9 8 7 6 5 4 3

Printed in Belgium

www.northsouth.com

HANS CHRISTIAN ANDERSEN

THUMBELINE

ILLUSTRATED BY LISBETH ZWERGER

TRANSLATED BY ANTHEA BELL

NorthSouth
New York / London

Once upon a time there was a woman who longed to have a tiny child of her own, but she had no idea where to get one. So she went to see an old witch, and asked her, "I do so long to have a little child; won't you tell me where I can get one?"

"Oh, we'll soon deal with that," said the witch. "Here, take this barleycorn. It is no ordinary barleycorn, not the kind that grows in the farmer's fields or is given to the chickens to eat! Put it in a flowerpot, and you will see what you will see!"

"Thank you kindly," said the woman, and she gave the witch some money. Then she went home and planted the barleycorn, and it instantly grew into a large and beautiful flower. The flower looked just like a tulip, but its petals were tightly furled as if it were still in bud.

"What a lovely flower!" said the woman, and she kissed its beautiful red-and-yellow petals. But the moment that she kissed it, the flower burst open with a loud snap. Anyone could see it really was a tulip, but there was a tiny little girl, very delicate and sweet, sitting in the middle of the flower on its green center. She was no bigger than your thumb, and so she was called Thumbeline.

She was given a prettily lacquered walnut shell for a cradle, and she lay there on blue violet-petals, with a rose petal coverlet over her. She slept in her cradle by night, but by day she played on the table. The woman had put a plate on the table, holding a wreath of flowers with their stalks hanging down in the water and a big tulip petal floating on top of it. Thumbeline could ferry herself from one side of the plate to the other on this petal, using two white horsehairs for oars. It was a pretty sight. She could sing, too, in the sweetest, loveliest voice that ever was heard.

One night as she lay in her pretty little bed, an ugly toad came hopping in through the window, which had a broken pane. The toad was big and ugly and wet. She hopped right over to the table where Thumbeline lay asleep under her red rose petal.

"What a nice wife she would make for my son!" said the toad. And she picked up the walnut shell where Thumbeline lay asleep, and hopped away with it right through the broken pane and out into the garden.

There was a big broad stream running by. Its banks were all muddy and marshy, and the toad lived here with her son. Oh, dear, he was so ugly and nasty, and he looked just like his mother! All he could say when he saw the sweet little girl in her walnut shell was, "Croak! Croak! Croak, croak, croak!"

"Don't speak so loud, or you'll wake her," said the old mother toad. "She could still run away from us, for she's as light as swansdown. We will lay her on one of the big water-lily leaves on the stream. Little and light as she is, it will be like an island to her! Then she won't be able to run away from us while we clear out our best room down in the mud, where the pair of you are to keep house!"

There were a great many water lilies growing out in the stream, with broad green leaves that looked as if they were floating on top of the water. The leaf that was farthest away was the biggest one, too. The old mother toad swam out to this leaf and placed Thumbeline in her walnut shell on it.

The poor little thing woke up very early the next morning, and when she saw where she was, she began to weep bitterly, for there was water all around the big green leaf and she could not get to land at all.

The old toad was down in the mud, decking out her best room with reeds and yellow marsh marigold petals to make it pretty for her new daughter-in-law. Then she and her ugly son swam out to the leaf where Thumbeline lay. They were going to fetch her pretty bed and put it in the bridal chamber before she came over herself.

The old mother toad curtseyed low in the water to her, and said, "This is my son, who is to be your husband, and the two of you will live very comfortably together down in the mud!"

"Croak! Croak! Croak, croak, croak!" was all her son could find to say.

So then she picked up the pretty little bed and swam away with it. Thumbeline sat all alone on the green leaf, weeping because she did not want to live with the nasty toad or be married to her ugly son.

The little fishes swimming down in the water must have seen the toad and heard what she said, for they put their heads out to see the little girl for themselves. As soon as they set eyes on her, they loved her so much that they would have been very sorry to see her forced to go down and live with the ugly toad! No, that must never be! They clustered together in the water around the green stalk of the leaf on which she was sitting, and nibbled through it with their teeth. Then the leaf floated downstream with Thumbeline, far, far away, where the toad could not follow.

Thumbeline floated past a great many places, and the little birds perching in the bushes saw her and sang, "Oh, what a lovely little lady!" The leaf floated on and on with her, and so Thumbeline came to another country.

A pretty little white butterfly kept flying around Thumbeline and at last settled on the leaf, for it had taken a liking to the little girl. Thumbeline was very happy now. The toads could no longer get at her, and they were passing such pretty scenery. The sun shone on the water like glimmering gold, and as the leaf sped along even faster, Thumbeline took her sash and tied one end to the butterfly and the other to the leaf.

At that moment a big June beetle came flying up and saw her. He immediately clasped her slender waist with his claws and flew up into a tree with her. But the green leaf floated on downstream, taking the butterfly with it, for the butterfly was tied to the leaf and could not get away.

Oh, dear, how frightened poor Thumbeline was when the June beetle flew up into the tree with her. She was saddest of all because of the pretty white butterfly she tied to the leaf; if it could not get free now, it would starve to death! But the June beetle didn't care about that. He settled on the biggest green leaf in the tree with her, gave her nectar from the flowers to eat, and said she was very pretty, even if she was not in the least like a June beetle.

Then all the other June beetles who lived in that tree came visiting. They looked at Thumbeline, and the June beetle girls shrugged their feelers and said, "Why, she has only two legs—what a wretched sight!" "Oh, she has no feelers!" they said.

"And her waist is so slim! She looks just like a human being. How ugly she is!" said all the lady June beetles, and yet Thumbeline was very pretty indeed. Or so the June beetle who had caught her thought; but when all the others said she was ugly he ended up believing them, and did not want her anymore, so now she could go where she liked.

They flew down from the tree with her and put her on a daisy. She cried, because she was so ugly that the June beetles didn't want anything to do with her—and yet she was the prettiest thing you ever saw, as fine and bright as the loveliest of rose petals.

All summer long poor Thumbeline lived alone in the great wood. She wove herself a bed of grass blades and slung it under a big burdock leaf, so that the rain could not get at her; she squeezed nectar from the flowers and ate it, and she drank the dew that stood on the leaves every morning.

So summer and fall passed by, but then winter came, and the winter was long and cold. All the birds who had sung so beautifully for her flew away. The trees and the flowers faded, the big burdock leaf under which she had slept curled up and became a yellow, withered stem, and she was terribly cold, for her clothes were worn out. Poor little Thumbeline was so tiny and delicate that she was in danger of freezing to death. It began to snow, and every snowflake that fell on her was like a whole shovelful being thrown on one of us, since we are big folk, and she was only the size of your thumb. So she wrapped herself in a dead leaf, but there was no warmth in it, and she shivered with the cold.

Beyond the wood to which she had come there lay a big wheatfield, but the wheat had been cut long ago, and there was only bare, dry stubble on the frozen ground. The stubble was like a forest to Thumbeline as she walked through it, trembling dreadfully with cold.

At last she came to the fieldmouse's door, a little hole down among the stubble. The fieldmouse was very warm and comfortable living down there, with a whole room full of grain, and a fine kitchen and a larder. Poor Thumbeline stood at her door like a beggar girl, asking for a tiny piece of barleycorn, because she had had nothing at all to eat for two days.

"You poor little thing," said the fieldmouse, who was a good old creature at heart. "Come into my nice warm room and share my meal!" She took a fancy to Thumbeline, and told her, "You can stay the winter with me if you like, but you must keep my house clean and tell me stories. I'm very fond of stories."

So Thumbeline did as the good old fieldmouse asked, and she was very comfortable indeed.

"We'll soon be having a visitor," said the fieldmouse. "My neighbor usually comes to visit me every day of the week. He is even better off then me, and has a finer house than mine, with great big rooms to live in, and he wears a fine black velvet fur coat. If you could only marry him, you'd be well provided for. But he can't see, so you must tell him the very best stories you know!"

However, Thumbeline did not like this idea. She didn't want to marry the neighbor a bit, for he was a mole.

And so he came visiting, in his black velvet coat. The fieldmouse said he was very rich and very clever, and his property was over twenty times bigger than hers. The mole knew all sorts of things, but he could not bear the sun and the pretty flowers, and he never spoke well of them because he had never seen them. Thumbeline had to sing for him, so she sang "Ladybird, ladybird, fly away home," and "The monk in the meadow."

The mole fell in love with her for her pretty voice, but he said nothing yet, for he was a very cautious man. Recently he had dug a long passage through the earth from his house to the fieldmouse's, and he said the fieldmouse and Thumbeline could walk there whenever they liked. He told them not to be afraid of the dead bird lying in the passage. The bird was a whole one with beak and feathers and all; it could only just have died when winter came, and now it lay buried on the spot where he had dug his own passage.

The mole took a piece of rotten wood in his mouth, for rotten wood shines like fire in the dark, and went ahead to light the way down the long, dark passage for them. When they came to the place where the dead bird lay, the mole put his big nose against the roof and pushed up the earth, making a large hole so that the light could shine in. In the middle of the floor lay a dead swallow, its beautiful wings close to its sides, its legs and head tucked into its feathers. Poor bird, it must surely have died of cold.

Thumbeline felt very sorry for it, for she loved all the little birds dearly. They had sung and chirped for her so prettily all summer long. But the mole gave it a kick with his stumpy leg and said, "That's the end of all his twittering! How miserable to be born a bird! Thank heaven none of my own children will be birds—all a bird can do is sing, and then starve to death in the winter."

"You are a sensible man, and you may well say so," agreed the fieldmouse. "What reward does a bird get for his singing when winter comes? It must starve and freeze, and yet birds are thought so wonderful!"

Thumbeline said nothing, but when the other two had turned their backs on the bird she bent down, parted the feathers over its head and kissed its closed eyes. Perhaps this was the very bird that sang so beautifully for me in summer, she thought. How happy the dear, pretty bird made me then!

The mole stopped up the hole through which daylight shone in and took the ladies home again. That night, however, Thumbeline could not sleep. She made a beautiful big blanket out of hay, carried it down and wrapped it around the pretty bird. She tucked some soft cotton she had found in the fieldmouse's house close to the bird's sides, to make him a warm place to lie in the cold earth.

"Goodbye, you lovely little bird!" she said. "Goodbye, and thank you for your beautiful songs in summer, when all the trees were green and the sun shone so warmly!" And she laid her head on the bird's breast; but then she had a shock, for it felt as if something were beating inside. It was the bird's heart! The swallow was not dead, only unconscious, and now that he was warmer, he was coming back to life.

Swallows all fly to the warm countries in autumn, but if one of them lingers too long it freezes, falls to the ground and lies where it has fallen as if dead, and the cold snow covers it up.

Thumbeline was trembling with fright, for as she was only the size of your thumb, the bird looked gigantic to her. But she plucked up her courage, tucked the cotton closer around the poor swallow, and fetched a mint leaf she herself had been using as a coverlet to lay over the bird's head.

Next night she slipped down to see him again. He was awake, but so tired he could only open his eyes for a moment, to see Thumbeline standing there with a piece of rotten wood in her hand, since she had no other lantern.

"Thank you, my dear, sweet child, thank you!" said the sick swallow. "I am so nice and warm now! I'll soon have my strength back, and then I'll be able to fly out into the warm sunshine again!"

"Oh, but it's so cold outside now!" she said. "It is snowing and freezing! You must stay warm in bed, and I'll look after you!"

She brought the swallow water in a flower petal. He drank it, and told her he had hurt a wing on a thorn bush, so that he could not fly as fast as the other swallows when they all went far, far away to the warm countries. At last he had fallen to the ground, and that was all he knew. He had no idea how he had come to be under the ground.

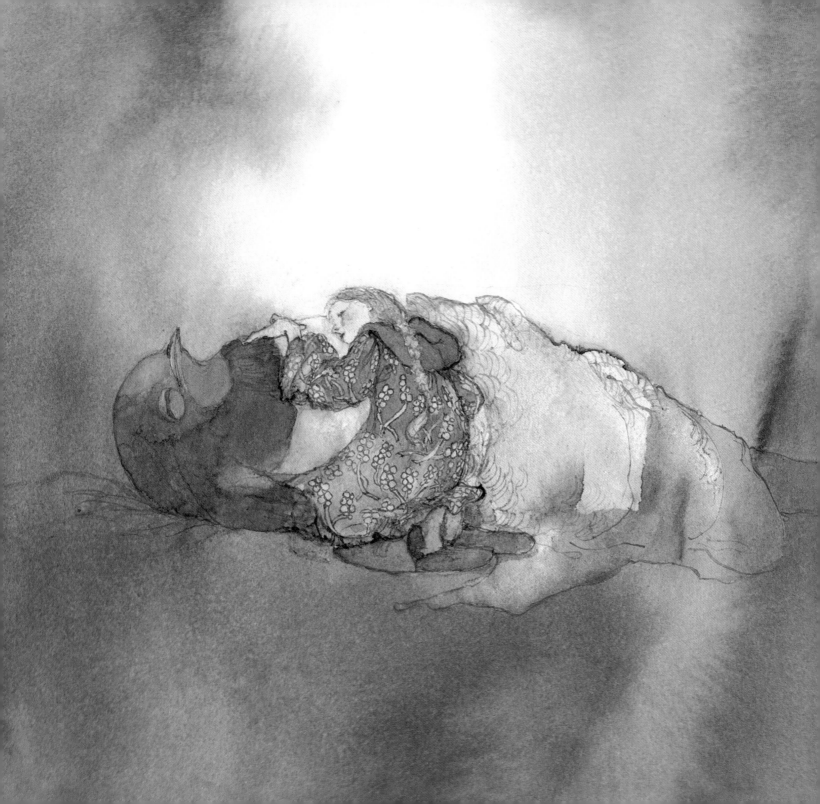

So he stayed down there all winter, and Thumbeline was good to him, and loved him very much. She did not let the mole or the fieldmouse know anything about it, because they would not care about helping the poor sick swallow.

As soon as spring came, and the sun's rays warmed the earth, the swallow said goodbye to Thumbeline. She opened up the hole the mole had made in the roof overhead. The sun shone in on them so beautifully, and the swallow asked if she would like to come with him. He said she could sit on his back, and they would fly far away into the green wood. But Thumbeline knew it would hurt the old fieldmouse's feelings if she left like that.

"No," said Thumbeline, "I can't go."

"Goodbye, goodbye, you sweet, good girl," said the swallow, and he flew out into the sunshine. Thumbeline watched him go, and tears came to her eyes, because she loved the poor swallow so much.

"Tweet! Tweet!" sang the bird, and he flew away into the green wood.

Thumbeline was very sad. She was not allowed to go out into the warm sunlight. The seedcorn sown in the field above the mousehole was growing tall now, and it was like a thick forest to a poor little girl only as big as your thumb.

"You must spend the summer sewing your trousseau!" the fieldmouse told her, for Neighbor Mole, who was so tedious but had a black velvet fur coat, had asked for her hand in marriage. "You will have both wool and linen to wear, and underclothes and household linen, when you are married to the mole."

So Thumbeline had to sit at the distaff and spin, and the fieldmouse hired four spiders to come, too, and spin and weave by day and by night.

Every evening, the mole came visiting, and he always said that when the summer came to an end, and the sun was not as hot as it was now, when it baked the earth as hard as stone—yes, when summer was over, his wedding to Thumbeline would be held.

She did not like the thought of it at all, for she could not bear the tedious mole. Every morning at sunrise, and every evening at sunset, she would slip outside the door, and when the wind blew the ears of wheat apart so that she could see the blue sky, she thought how bright and lovely it was out here, and longed to see her old friend the swallow again. But the swallow did not come back. He had flown far away into the beautiful green wood.

When fall came, Thumbeline had her trousseau ready. "You are to be married in four weeks' time," the fieldmouse told her. But Thumbeline wept and said she did not want to marry the tiresome old mole.

"Fiddle-de-dee!" said the fieldmouse. "Don't be so stubborn, or I'll bite you with my white teeth! It's a very fine husband you are getting! Why, the queen herself does not own a black velvet fur coat the like of his. He has stores in his kitchen and his cellar, and you ought to thank Heaven for him!"

So the wedding was to take place. The mole had already come to fetch Thumbeline away to live with him deep down underground. They would never again come out to see the warm sun, for the mole could not stand sunshine. Poor child, she was very unhappy to have to say goodbye to the beautiful sun. While she was living with the fieldmouse she had at least been able to step outside the door and see it.

"Goodbye, bright sun!" she cried, stretching her arms up into the air, and she walked a little way beyond the fieldmouse's hole, for the wheat had been reaped now and there was nothing left but dry stubble. "Goodbye, goodbye!" she said, putting her arms around a little red flower that grew there. "Give my love to my dear swallow, if you see him!"

"Tweet! Tweet!" sang a voice overhead at that very moment. She looked up, and it was the swallow flying by. He was delighted to see Thumbeline. She told him how little she liked the thought of marrying the ugly mole, and going to live underground where the sun never shone. She had to shed tears—she could not help it.

"The cold winter is coming," said the swallow. "I'm flying away to the warm countries. Would you like to come with me? You can sit on my back. Just tie yourself on with your sash and we'll fly away from the ugly mole and his dark house, far away over the mountains to the warm countries, where the sun shines more beautifully than it does here, and where it is always summer and there are lovely flowers. Do fly away with me, dear little Thumbeline who saved my life when I lay frozen in the dark, underground!"

"Oh, yes, I'll come with you!" said Thumbeline, and she sat on the bird's back, with her feet on his outspread wings, and tied her sash to one of his strongest feathers. Then the swallow flew high up into the air, over the woods and over the water, over the high mountains where snow lies all the year round. Thumbeline was freezing in the cold air, but she crept in among the bird's warm feathers, and just put her little head out to see all the wonders down below.

So they came to the warm countries. The sun shone much more brightly there than it does here, the sky was twice as high, and the most beautiful green and blue grapes grew all along the ditches and the hedges. The woods were full of oranges and lemons, the air was fragrant with myrtle and mint, and the prettiest of children ran down the road playing with big, bright butterflies.

But still the swallow flew on, and everything became even more beautiful. A shining white marble castle of the olden days stood beneath splendid green trees by the side of a blue lake. Vines clambered around its tall columns, and there were a great many swallows' nests up at the top. One of them belonged to the swallow who was carrying Thumbeline.

"Here is my home," said the swallow. "But if you'd like to choose one of the magnificent flowers growing down below for yourself, I'll put you into it, and you will live there as comfortably as ever you could wish!"

"Oh, that would be wonderful!" she said, clapping her little hands.

One big white marble column had fallen to the ground and was broken into three, but the loveliest big, white flowers grew among its pieces. The swallow flew down with Thumbeline and put her on the wide petals of one of these flowers. How surprised she was to see a little man sitting in the middle of the flower! He was as pale and clear as if he were made of glass, and he wore the dearest little gold crown on his head, and had the loveliest bright wings on his shoulders. He was the spirit of the flower, and he himself was no bigger than Thumbeline. There was a little man or woman like him living in every flower, but he was the king of them all.

"Oh, how handsome he is!" Thumbeline whispered to the swallow.

As for the little prince, he was quite frightened of the swallow, for the bird was enormous compared to his own small and delicate self. But when he set eyes on Thumbeline he was delighted, for she was the most beautiful girl he had ever seen. So he took the gold crown off his head, and put it on hers, and asked her name. Then he asked if she would be his wife and become the queen of all the flowers! Well, this was a nicer sort of husband than the toad's son, or the mole with his black velvet fur coat. So she said "Yes" to the handsome prince.

Then a little lady or a little gentleman came out of every flower, all so pretty that it was a joy to see them. They all brought Thumbeline presents, and the best of all was a pair of lovely wings from a big white fly. The wings were fastened to Thumbeline's back, and now she, too, could fly from flower to flower.

How happy they all were! The swallow sat in his nest, and sang for them with all his might. But he was sad at heart, for he loved Thumbeline, and never wanted to part with her.

"You must not be called Thumbeline anymore," said the Prince of the Flowers. "It's an ugly name, and you so beautiful. We will call you Maia!"

"Goodbye, goodbye!" said the swallow, for it had come to be the season for him to fly away from the warm countries, far away and back again to Denmark. There he had a little nest above the window where the man who tells fairy tales lives. The swallow sang, "Tweet, tweet!" to the man, and that is how we come to know the whole story.

As a young art student in Vienna in 1972, Lisbeth Zwerger freely told others that she wanted to illustrate books. She recalls, "I was often told, or rather warned, of the difficulties involved in finding work, and criticized for not being 'modern' enough, which naturally left me feeling totally confused, not really knowing what direction my work should take. In fact, I almost stopped drawing completely, limiting myself to the occasional black and white ink drawing."

Fortunately for the world of children's literature, one day a friend showed her a book illustrated by Arthur Rackham. "Suddenly something seemed to click, my doubts vanished, and I felt inspired to illustrate again." In the years since then, Lisbeth Zwerger has illustrated more than twenty classical stories—stories with as much history and charm and character as her native Vienna.

"With each new project she shapes her talent to suit the words rather than use them simply as a showcase. Speaking of a favorite English illustrator she has commented on finding 'the perfect balance literature and art are capable of reaching.' That is a balance found by very few of the very best illustrative artists. Lisbeth Zwerger is already among them." —*The New York Times*